This MAMMOTH belongs to

_____

_____

_____

To all the
good friends
of Miss Bilberry

Miss Bilberry's New House

Emma Chichester Clark

MAMMOTH

$\mathcal{M}$iss Bilberry lived in a pale yellow house with a fine view of the mountains. She had a dog whose name was Cecilie, a cat called Chester, and two birds called Chitty and Chatty.

Every day, Miss Bilberry jumped out of bed, brushed her teeth, dressed, put on her hat and had breakfast in the shade of the broad-leaved tree, looking out at the blue mountains.

After breakfast she swept the path with a thin reed broom and fed the birds and animals. She watered the flowers and vegetables growing in her garden and had a light lunch on the verandah.

Then she had a nap in her hammock between two swaying palms,
and supper under the stars. Sometimes she played her violin
and sang a few songs, and then she went to bed.

It was a lovely life, and if it weren't for
one thing, Miss Bilberry would have
been completely happy…

She just couldn't stop wondering whether
she might not be even happier if she lived on
the other side of the mountains. The more she looked,
the more she wondered.

One day, Miss Bilberry jumped out of bed and said,
"Everybody up! Today's the day for moving house!
Let's start packing!"
They filled all their boxes, baskets and bags and put
everything on to a wobbly old cart.

They waved goodbye to the house and the garden, the
broad-leaved tree and the two swaying palms, and set
off towards the blue mountains.
"Oh, I'm so excited," cried Miss Bilberry, "I just can't wait
to get to the other side!"

They walked and pushed the cart for many miles, through fields

and forests,

through rain

and sunshine,

uphill,

and downhill.

In some places the flowers were taller than Miss Bilberry!
They could hardly see where they were going.
"This is the wrong way," snarled Chester.
"No it isn't," snapped Cecilie.
They argued for hours. It nearly drove Miss Bilberry mad.

Miss Bilberry climbed a tree, but she still wasn't sure where they
were. Should they go left or right? She had no idea at all.
"Do stop quarrelling, you two," she said, "everything is going to
be fine when we get to the other side."

On and on they went, through days and nights. The further they went, the more lost they became, and it felt as though the journey would never end.

"I want to go back to our lovely old house," said Cecilie.
"I want to go home," moaned Chester.
"If you don't stop grumbling I'll leave you right here!"
said Miss Bilberry.

Miss Bilberry sent Chitty and Chatty ahead. They could fly above the trees and see where to go next, but they weren't very clever, so they usually forgot where they'd been.

"They're *hopeless*!" snarled Chester. "We could sit here for days
before they find us again. I expect we're going round in circles."
But one day, Chitty and Chatty returned, their shrieks
echoing all over the forest.
"We're there! We're there! Come and see!
A lovely house! Come and see."

And there it was...
"Oh my!" gasped Miss Bilberry. "Oh my, oh my!
It's perfection. It's just as I thought it would be!"

"Thank goodness for that," sighed Chester. It wasn't very far to
go, just a few fields, down a hill and through a meadow.

They ran all the way.   They unloaded the cart and
emptied the bags.   Chester sniffed the air and looked puzzled.
"It's strange," he thought, "but I feel as if I've been here before."

Miss Bilberry was so tired that she slept all afternoon in the hammock that she strung between two swaying palms, exactly like before. Then she made a stew from the vegetables growing in the garden and they all began to feel better.

Each morning the sun shone. Miss Bilberry smiled as she leapt out of bed, and her life seemed better than ever. Her breakfast was more delicious, the mountains more beautiful, the animals more cheerful. They were all happier than ever before.

Only Chester gave Miss Bilberry a funny look now and
then, but she never knew what he was thinking. Sometimes she
lay awake and remembered their long journey, it must have been
about a hundred miles. She was pleased with the way things had
turned out, even though some quite peculiar things had
happened lately...

The first was that Miss Bilberry had found her very own old
tooth-brush in the bathroom. Then she found Cecilie's bowl
in the garden, and a very old sock she'd been knitting before they
moved was under her bed. How did they get there?
Miss Bilberry gazed out at the mountains and wondered.
Do you know what she was wondering?

Chester, the clever cat, watched her and smiled to himself. You have probably guessed by now that Miss Bilberry's new house was not a new house at all, but Miss Bilberry... well, if she did know, she didn't say a word to anybody, and they all lived there happily ever after.

The end

First published in Great Britain 1993
by Methuen Children's Books Ltd
Published 1995 by Mammoth
an imprint of Reed Books Ltd
Michelin House, 81 Fulham Road, London SW3 6RB
and Auckland, Melbourne, Singapore and Toronto

Copyright © Emma Chichester Clark 1993

ISBN 0 7497 2502 8

A CIP catalogue record for this title
is available from the British Library

Produced by Mandarin Offset Ltd
Printed and bound in Hong Kong